www.enchantedlionbooks.com

Text copyright © 2016 by Michaël Escoffier
Illustrations copyright © 2016 by Kris Di Giacomo

First edition published in 2016 by Enchanted Lion Books,
351 Van Brunt Street, Brooklyn, NY 11231

ISBN 978-1-59270-201-5

Design and layout: Kris Di Giacomo
Printed in China by R. R. Donnelley Print Solutions

10 9 8 7 6 5 4 3 2 1

Have you Seen my Trumpet?

written by Michaël Escoffier

illustrated by Kris Di Giacomo

ENCHANTED LION BOOKS
NEW YORK

Who is playing frisbee?

Who is blowing
a dandelion?

Who is being
selfish?

Excuse me,
Have you seen
my Trumpet?

No,
I haven't.

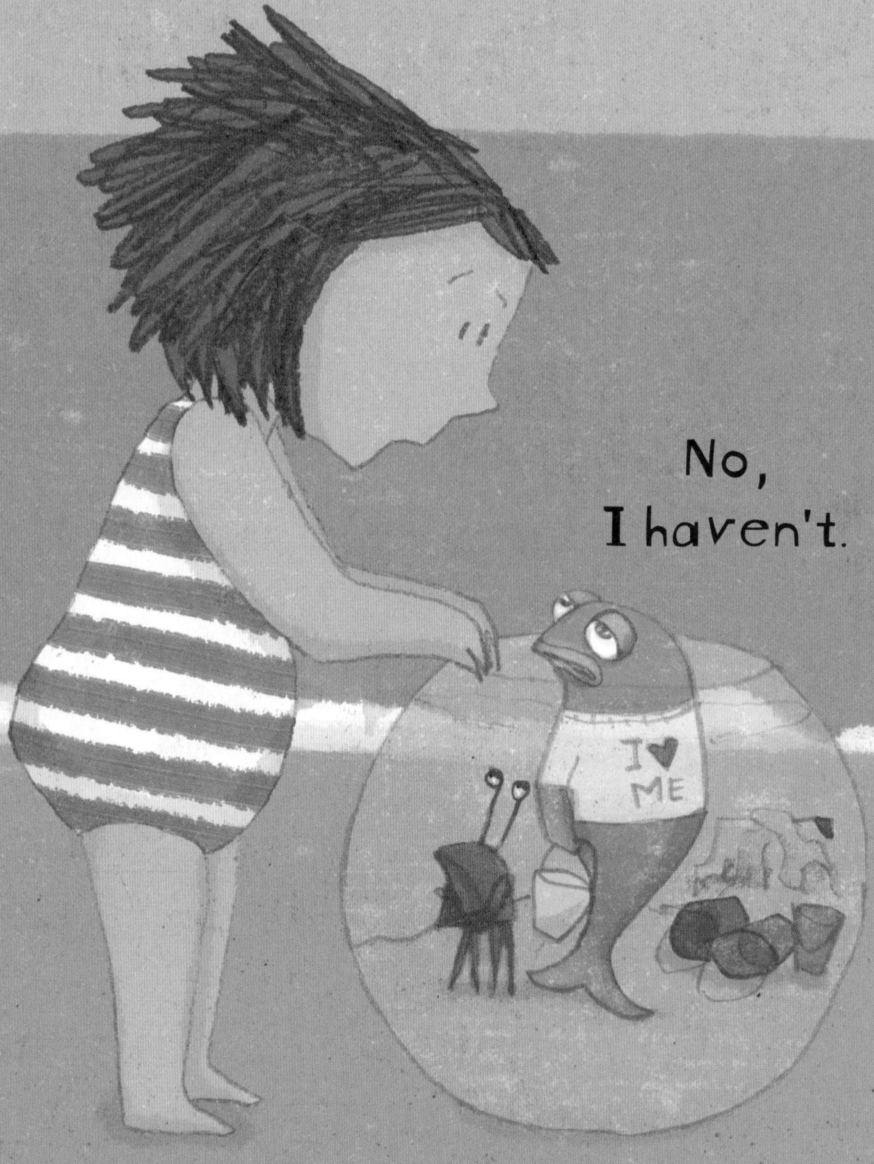

Who thinks it's too crowded?

Who is chasing the pigeon?

Who is in the bathroom?

Excuse me,
have you seen
my Trumpet?

No I haven't!
Go away!
Get out!

Who is in the kayak?

Who is at the wheel?

Who is shouting gruffly?

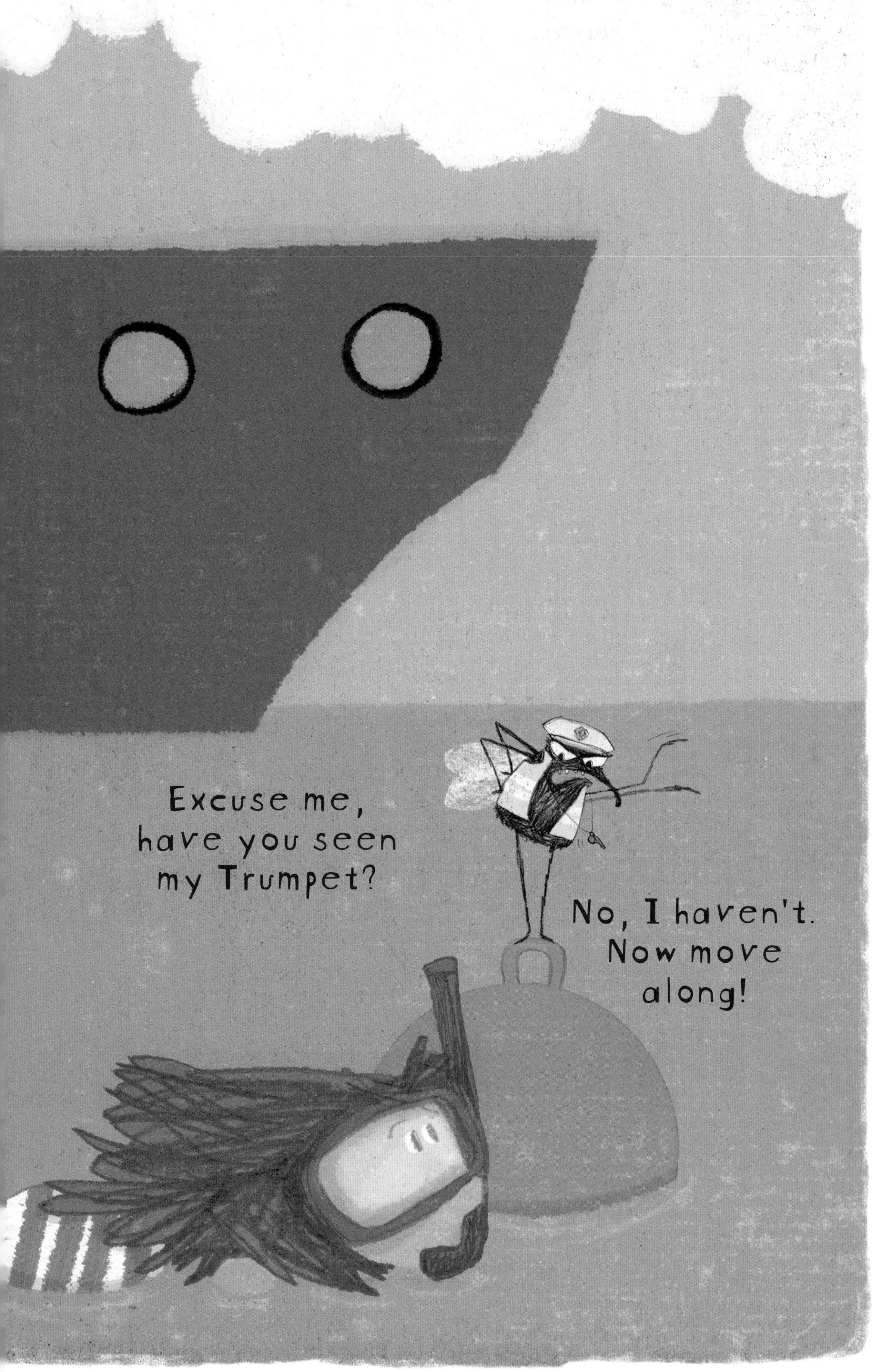
Excuse me, have you seen my Trumpet?
No, I haven't. Now move along!

Who loves
guacamole?

Who fell into the fishbowl?

Who is robbing the elephant?